YOU CALL THE PLAY:

FOOTBALL

Quarterback Attack

BY PETER STRUPP

A Sports Illustrated For Kids Book

BANTAM BOOKS

TORONTO • NEW YORK • LONDON • SYDNEY • AUCKLAND

You Call the Play: Football/Quarterback Attack
A Bantam Book/July 1995

SPORTS ILLUSTRATED FOR KIDS and are registered
trademarks of Time Inc.
SPORTS ILLUSTRATED FOR KIDS BOOKS are published in
cooperation with Bantam Doubleday Dell Publishing Group, Inc. under
license from Time Inc.

Cover and interior design by Miriam Dustin
Illustrations by Daryl Cagle
Cover photographs: Louis DeLuca (Troy Aikman), Bill Frakes (crowd)

ISBN 0-553-48312-9

Published simultaneously in the United States and Canada

Bantam Books are published by Bantam Books, a division of Bantam
Doubleday Dell Publishing Group, Inc. Its trademark, consisting of the
words "Bantam Books" and the portrayal of a rooster, is Registered in U.S.
Patent and Trademark Office and in other countries. Marca Registrada.
Bantam Books, 1540 Broadway, New York, New York, 10036.

PRINTED IN THE UNITED STATES OF AMERICA

CWO 10 9 8 7 6 5 4 3

YOU CALL THE PLAY: FOOTBALL is more than a football book that you read. It's a football *game* book that you can play! You are the Kid, the rookie quarterback of the Wildcats, and today is Super Sunday, the championship game of pro football. You are taking on the defending champion Grizzlies.

You won't read this book straight through like you would a normal story. Instead, you'll come face-to-face with all the tough offensive decisions of a game and be given a choice of which play to call. After you choose, follow the instructions at the bottom of the page. The game announcers will tell you how the play turns out.

Each decision you make will lead to a new situation and will eventually help determine the outcome of the game. There are 29 different endings, so you can play the game again and again.

Before you start, look at the running plays on page 7, the pass patterns on page 8, and the defensive formations on page 9. These will help you decide which plays to call. You can check back to these pages throughout the game to help you make your calls.

Okay, now buckle your chinstrap and head out the tunnel. They're announcing the starting lineups!

THE PLACE: The Metro Bowl, in sunny Coastal City. The temperature at the 4 p.m. kickoff is an ideal 70 degrees, and the natural grass field is in perfect condition. The game is a sellout, of course, and the 75,920 fans are pretty evenly split between Wildcat "howlers" and Grizzly "growlers."

ROSTERS

WILDCATS (This is your team, Kid.)

Earl "Sheepy" Goodwin, head coach. Sheepy has been coaching for 25 years, all with the Wildcats. They call him "Sheepy" for his curly hair. (It turned white after his first season running the Wildcats.) Sheepy isn't into gimmicks — he believes that you win games by sticking to basics. But he will listen to new ideas and enjoys working with young quarterbacks.

THE STARTING LINEUPS

No.	Name	Pos.	Ht.	Wt.	Years
12	**The Kid**	QB	6' 1"	195	R

This is you, the first rookie in league history to lead his team to the championship game. You can read defenses and you have the patience in the pocket to let a pass play develop, but you're not afraid to run with the ball when you have to.

No.	Name	Pos.	Ht.	Wt.	Years
32	**Franco Turner**	FB	6' 1"	245	5

Franco is a workhorse. He rushed for 1,000 yards this season and can catch the ball out of the backfield. He was named all-conference.

No.	Name	Pos.	Ht.	Wt.	Years
40	**Ray Rivera**	HB	5' 11"	200	3

A strong blocker for a little man, Ray gives the Wildcats speed on draw and trap plays. He is also a good pass receiver.

No.	Name	Pos.	Ht.	Wt.	Years
88	**Courtney Buckets**	RWR	6' 4"	220	4

Courtney has been named all-pro in each of his first four seasons. He has the speed and height to catch almost anything. But he always draws double coverage.

No.	Name	Pos.	Ht.	Wt.	Years
89	Raj Sanders	LWR	6' 0"	180	R

Raj is not the same deep threat as Courtney, but he knows how to find holes in the pass defense.

| 81 | Terry Warren | WR | 6' 1" | 190 | 13 |

The "Old Man" runs pass routes better than anyone. He can sneak into a game and come up with a big catch.

| 85 | Bobby Lardelle | TE | 6' 3" | 260 | 9 |

Once an overweight youngster, Bobby blossomed into a fine blocking tight end with great hands. He's quick, but no burner.

| 2 | Ian Wallace | K | 5' 9" | 150 | 12 |

"Old Reliable" has been splitting uprights since the day he moved here from England. But he strained the hamstring muscle in his right leg in the playoffs.

| 3 | Clark Hashimoto | P | 5' 11" | 170 | 5 |

Like most punters, Clark gets around: The Wildcats are his fifth team in five seasons. But he has been long, high, and accurate with his punts all year.

| 79 | Todd Schumacher | C | 6' 4" | 280 | 7 |

"The Rock," as Todd is called by teammates, will give you all-conference protection against the blitz.

| 77 | Bud Rooney | RG | 6' 2" | 280 | 9 |

Bud has been in and out all year with injuries. Some say he's lost a step.

| 76 | Larry Chapter | LG | 6' 3" | 290 | 10 |

A great pulling guard on the sweep, Larry is only so-so on pass protection.

| 70 | Wilson Parker | RT | 6' 4" | 280 | 6 |

Wilson is an all-pro drive-blocker on the sweep, and a brick wall on the pass.

| 71 | Eric Stern | LT | 6' 1" | 270 | 5 |

Small for the line, Eric makes up for his size with guts.

GRIZZLIES (THIS IS YOUR OPPONENT.)

Jack Rusk, head coach. This former linebacker believes that defense alone can win games. He developed the Grizzlies' "Purple Wallop" defense — the toughest in the league.

THE DEFENSIVE LINEUP

No.	Name	Pos.	Ht.	Wt.	Years
50	Brad Tacker	MLB	6' 1"	240	6

The Grizzly captain is smart, fast, mean, and all-pro.

55	Andy Lee	OLB	6' 2"	210	2

Overshadowed by Tacker, Lee blitzes well from the weak side.

66	Hank Stubblefield	OLB	6' 2"	235	7

This all-conference performer is slowed by a playoff injury.

75	Rusty Kunkel	DT	6' 0"	280	4

Kunkel is great at the sack, but he can be fooled on the run.

74	Olaf Hemingway	DT	6' 2"	300	11

The biggest Grizzly likes to "stay at home" to stop the run.

68	Herb Grount	DE	6' 3"	275	8

Grount is a brutal pass rusher, but slow in chasing runners.

69	Harvey Beardsley	DE	6' 4"	290	9

The "Gentleman Giant" led the league in sacks.

42	Ronnie Pepperidge	CB	5' 11"	195	2

Fast but green, Pepperidge will play mostly on the weak side.

40	O.B. Ballard	CB	6' 0"	205	4

The all-conference back provides flawless strongside coverage.

33	Kevin Conn	S	6' 1"	200	5

Also all-conference, Conn covers deep like a blanket.

35	Keith Jaeger	S	6' 2"	215	7

Jaeger is not only an all-pro, he may be the best ever.

39	Emmitt Hood	NB	6' 0"	195	R

A promising rookie, Hood comes in for the nickel defense.

OFFENSIVE PLAYS

RUNNING LANES

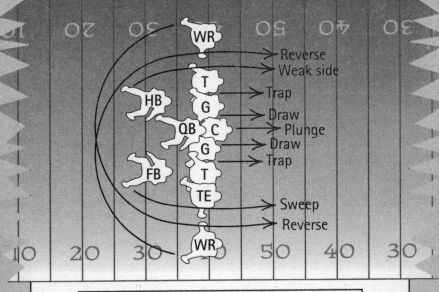

Wide Receiver	WR	Center	C
Tackle	T	Fullback	FB
Guard	G	Quarterback	QB
Halfback	HB	Tight End	TE

 The Wildcats wear white

The Grizzlies wear black

PASS PATTERNS

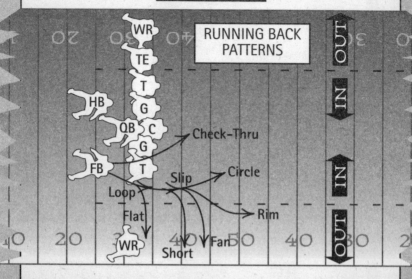

RUNNING BACK PATTERNS

Check-Thru
Circle
Slip
Loop
Rim
Flat
Short
Fan

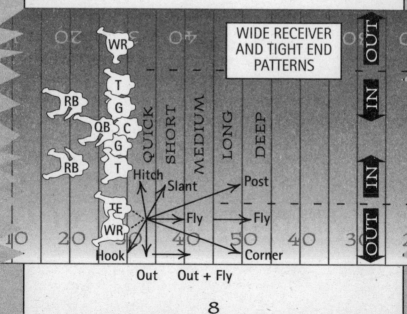

WIDE RECEIVER AND TIGHT END PATTERNS

QUICK
SHORT
MEDIUM
LONG
DEEP

Hitch
Slant
Post
Fly
Fly
Hook
Corner
Out
Out + Fly

8

DEFENSIVE FORMATIONS

Blitz: Linebackers or safeties will rush, trying to sack you.

Man-to-man: Each defensive back is responsible for a receiver.

Nickel: A linebacker is replaced by a fifth defensive back.

Prevent: Defense plays deep to protect against a long gain.

Stacked Line: Linebackers step up to the line to stop the run.

NICKEL DEFENSE

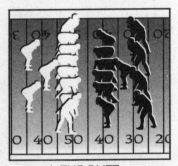

THE BLITZ

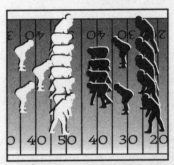

PREVENT DEFENSE

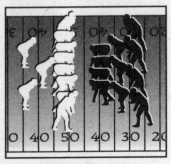

MAN-TO-MAN

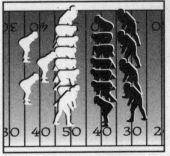

STACKED LINE

9

"Ooh boy, what a day for a football game! This is Don Dewright along with Hall of Famer Al Spooner, and it is our privilege to bring to you this year's pro football championship game. And Al, this game between the Wildcats and the Grizzlies has the makings of one of the all-time classics!"

"You got that, Don! We're going to see some real smash-mouth football here today at the Metro Bowl!"

"There are some great matchups between the Wildcat offense and the Grizzly defense, Al."

"Yes, Don, but the key matchup is between the two play-callers on the field: the Kid at quarterback for the Wildcats versus the leader of this Grizzly defense, linebacker Brad Tacker. It's the all-pro veteran against the up-and-coming Kid, and may the smarter player win!"

The Wildcats win the coin toss and elect to receive. The opening kickoff sails out of the end zone, and you take over at your own 20-yard line. A 2-yard run by Franco Turner and a 6-yard catch by Courtney Buckets gives you a third down and two yards to go for the first down from your 28.

"Now, the Wildcats are in their huddle, Al. They have to get the first down to keep the drive alive."

Down: 3
To Go: 2
Ball on: own 28
Time: 13:35
Defense: Man-to-Man

The Wildcats wear white
The Grizzlies wear black

"So, what are we going to do, Boss?"

That's your center, Todd Schumacher. He's always trying to keep you loose. This is the first important play of the game. Let's see . . . .

With this short yardage, the Grizzlies might be looking for the run. So you could send Courtney Buckets deep to clear out the defensive backs from the short right side of the field and then pass to Franco Turner on a *slip right*. Then again, Brad Tacker might pick up on it and be all over Franco.

Left guard Larry Chapter and left tackle Eric Stern looked good blocking Grizzly defensive tackle Rusty Kunkel and defensive end Herb Grount on the first two plays, so it might make more sense to hand off to Ray Rivera on a *trap left*.

THE KID

- To run a trap left, turn to page 12.
- To pass on a slip right, turn to page 54.

11

"The Kid steps up to the center. Brad Tacker is shouting at the Grizzly linebackers and defensive secondary to play closer to the line. The Kid calls the signals, then hands off to Ray Rivera running left. He's tackled by linebacker Andy Lee at the line for no gain. What happened there, Al Spooner?"

"Simple trap play, Don. But the Grizzlies were expecting the run. Eric Stern and Larry Chapter handled the Grizzly linemen well enough, but there wasn't anyone to block Lee!"

"And now the Wildcats face fourth and 2. Here comes Clark Hashimoto in to punt."

The Grizzlies score on their next possession to take a 7–0 lead. The two teams exchange possessions until the Wildcats mount a drive toward the end of the half. You move the team down the field to the Grizzly 35-yard line, where you now face a second down and 1 yard to go for the first down.

"There's the two-minute warning, Al. But the Kid has time to put some points on the board."

"Don, Andy Lee is leaving the game and Emmitt Hood, the Grizzlies' fifth defensive back, is coming in. The Grizzlies will be in their *nickel* defense to protect against the pass."

Quarter: 2   Wildcats 0, Grizzlies 7

Down: 2
To Go: 1
Ball on: Their 35
Time: 2:00
Defense: Nickel

This is great, Kid! You have plenty of time, you only need a yard for the first down, and you have three downs to get it. You can try almost anything.

Maybe you should try for the touchdown with a long pass right now. If it's incomplete, the clock will stop and there will be two more downs to get the first down. Courtney Buckets is the player to send on a long *corner* route.

Then again, the Grizzlies are in their nickel formation, with an extra back in the secondary and with one less linebacker. They're looking for the pass. Maybe a run to the *weak side* (that's the side the tight end is not lined up on; his side is the *strong side*) would be better — not as many yards, but safer. Make the call, Kid!

- To pass deep, turn to page 14.
- To try a weakside run, turn to page 24.

13

"Here we go, Al Spooner! The Grizzlies are in their nickel formation. Here's the snap. The Kid drops back in the pocket, Buckets and Sanders are both going long. Buckets has double coverage! The Kid throws. It's deep to Buckets and it's . . . picked off! Safety Keith Jaeger makes the interception! He returns it to the 20 . . . the 25. He cuts back and picks up blockers. He's to the 40 . . . the 45 . . . and Ray Rivera takes him down at midfield."

"That was a mistake, Don. An offense just shouldn't try to go right at a defense's strength."

The Grizzlies drive the rest of the field to score another touchdown and finish the half leading, 14–0. The game moves to the second half. A Grizzly punt gives the Wildcats the ball on your own 35. Then, a penalty against the Grizzlies puts you in a first down and 5 situation.

"We're early in the third quarter, and the Wildcats have a great chance to get back into this game, Al Spooner. Here comes the Kid, leading the Wildcats up to the line of scrimmage."

"The Kid had better be careful here, Don. With a two touchdown lead, the Grizzlies can gamble on defense. Right now, they're showing *blitz*."

Quarter: 3   **Wildcats 0, Grizzlies 14**

Down: 1
To Go: 5
Ball on: Your 40
Time: 12:10
Defense: Blitz

You'd better check the defense before you take the snap. You might want to change the play at the line.

The two outside linebackers are lined up just outside of the defensive ends. It looks like a blitz is coming. Those Grizzlies would just love to rush six men against your five offensive linemen and tackle you for a loss.

You can beat the blitz with a quick pass. The cornerbacks and safeties will be tightly guarding the wide receivers. You could send tight end Bobby Lardelle over the middle on a short *slant* pass, but he'll have to get past the blitzing linebackers first.

You could also keep Bobby in to block the blitzers and try fullback Franco Turner on a *loop* right.

- To pass to the tight end, turn to page 18.
- To pass to the fullback, turn to page 16.

15

"The Wildcats line up at their own 40, Al. The Kid smells a blitz and calls an audible. Schumacher snaps the ball, and the Kid drops back into the pocket. Ray Rivera and Bobby Lardelle tie up Lee and Stubblefield just long enough for the Kid to lob the ball to Turner at the line of scrimmage. Turner runs to the 45, where he's tackled by Brad Tacker. First down, Wildcats!"

The Wildcat drive continues, ending in a 3-yard touchdown run by Franco Turner. But the Grizzly defense shuts down the Wildcat offense until the Wildcats launch a long drive in the last minutes of the game, still trailing, 14–7. You move the ball down to the Grizzly 20, where the drive stalls. You now face a fourth down and 12 yards to go with only 1:54 left to play.

"Okay, Al Spooner. This is the play of the game. The Wildcats have no timeouts. A field goal won't do anything for them. They need the touchdown to tie."

"The Grizzlies have their *nickel* pass defense in, Don, to protect against a pass into the end zone. Let's see what the Kid comes up with here. Does he go for the touchdown or the first down?"

Quarter: 4 **Wildcats 7, Grizzlies 14**
Down: 4
To Go: 12
Ball on: Their 20
Time: 1:54
Defense: Nickel

THE KID

This is it, Kid! Think fast — the clock is ticking! It's fourth and 12 on their 20 and they're in a nickel. You might be able to gamble for a touchdown with a pass to Courtney Buckets on a long *post* route to the end zone. But their defensive secondary will be pretty crowded back there.

Maybe you should send Courtney deep as a decoy. He'll attract a few defensive backs and then you can try a short pass to Ray Rivera on a *circle* left route. He might be able to dance his way to the first down. No time for a huddle. You'll make the call at the line of scrimmage. Go!

- To pass for the touchdown, turn to page 19.
- To pass for the first down, turn to page 20.

"These Grizzlies can't wait to get a piece of the Kid, Don. They're lining up to blitz."

"Let's see how the Kid deals with the challenge, Al. He takes the snap and drops back to pass . . . and here comes Stubblefield and Lee! Tacker is coming, too! The Kid tries to scramble, but he gets crunched by Stubblefield. . . ."

"That ball is loose out there, Don!"

"The Kid has fumbled! Tacker picks it up at the Wildcat 30! He's to the 20 . . . the 10 . . . nobody is going to catch him . . . touchdown, Grizzlies!"

"Mercy, mercy, mercy."

"This is turning into a rout, Al Spooner. What happened there?"

"Well, the Kid saw the blitz coming, but he didn't have time to get a pass to a receiver. He needed to unload the ball faster."

"And the extra point is good. It looks bad for the Wildcats now."

It's just not your day, Kid. With a three-touch-down lead, the Grizzlies can keep gambling on defense. They come up with fumbles and interceptions that lead to more easy points, and win 34–3.

GRIZZLIES WIN

18

"The clock is running, Al Spooner, 1:54 . . . 1:53 . . . the Wildcats are out of timeouts. Center Todd Schumacher snaps the ball to the Kid. The Kid drops back in the pocket, with no real pass rush coming from the Grizzly line. He looks downfield. He has Raj Sanders drawing double coverage on a medium fly, and Courtney Buckets breaking long on a post pattern. Bucket's got two Grizzlies surrounding him."

"The Kid isn't messing around with the first down! This is for the glory, baby!"

"The Kid unloads the ball long. Buckets, O.B. Ballard, and Keith Jaeger are all going up for it in the end zone, and it's . . . incomplete."

"That's the game, Donald. A heart-breaker for the Wildcats. For this big play, the Kid wanted to go to his main receiver, and the Grizzlies were ready. Outstanding defense by the Grizzlies all day."

"The Grizzlies hold on to that 14–7 lead, folks. Now all that's left is for the Grizzly defense to finish high-fiving each other and leave the field, so their offense can run out the clock."

GRIZZLIES WIN

"There is no tomorrow for the Wildcats, Al Spooner. The clock is at 1:53 and the Kid is calling signals at the line. Here's the snap, and both receivers are going long. The Kid looks deep . . . then tosses a short pass to Ray Rivera circling out of the backfield! It's complete at the 10. Rivera's got the first down! He picks up a block . . . he's going to score! Touchdown, Wildcats!"

"Baby, what a play! The Kid was patient, and that patience was rewarded."

"The extra point is good, and we've got a 14–14 game, with just 90 seconds left in regulation!"

On the following kickoff, Wildcat coach Sheepy Goodwin calls for an onside kick and it works! You take over on offense at your own 45 and move the ball into Grizzly territory. Now you face a second down and 8 on the Grizzly 42. There are only 25 seconds left before the game goes into overtime.

"Don, the Grizzlies are in their *prevent* defense to guard against the Kid trying a long pass. It looks like they are willing to give up a few short ones and run the clock down. They're planning on overtime."

Quarter: 4   **Wildcats 14, Grizzlies 14**
Down: 2
To Go: 8
Ball on: Their 42
Time: 0:25
Defense: Prevent

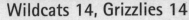

THE KID

You know something, Kid? Sheepy Goodwin is a crafty one. The Grizzlies are in a prevent defense, just making sure that nothing happens while they wait for the clock to run out and for overtime to begin. But Sheepy is signalling for you to pass. Raj Sanders has been drawing single coverage. The defense has been keying on Courtney Buckets. Maybe this is the time to send Raj deep.

Also, the entire Grizzly secondary is 15 yards back off the line of scrimmage. They're so worried about the touchdown that they'll give up the short gain. A pass to tight end Bobby Lardelle on a medium *out* pattern might get you into field goal range. Who wants overtime if you can win it right now? The clock is running so decide quickly!

- To pass deep to Raj Sanders, turn to page 22.
- To throw to the tight end, turn to page 23.

"Okay, Al Spooner, here we go! The Wildcats come up to the Grizzly 42 with 24 seconds to play, facing the Grizzlies deep prevent formation. Here's the snap."

"Hey, the Kid's taking it to them, Don! Raj Sanders and Courtney Buckets are both going deep . . . and both are being double-teamed."

"Here comes the ball, Al . . . and it's intercepted by Ronnie Pepperidge! The Grizzly cornerback returns it to the 20 . . . the 25 . . . he cuts across the middle of the field, picking up blockers! He's past the 35, with just one Wildcat tackler left to beat. *Pow!* Andy Lee takes out Franco Turner with a vicious block, and Ronnie Pepperidge is at midfield with 50 empty yards to go! Nobody's going to catch him! Touchdown, Grizzlies! The game is over! The final score is 21–14. What a finish!"

GRIZZLIES WIN

"The Wildcats line up at the Grizzly 42, with 24 seconds on the clock. The Grizzlies are in a deep prevent formation. Todd Schumacher snaps the ball. Buckets and Sanders are going deep, right into the coverage. Tight end Bobby Lardelle slips through the line, and the Kid spots him. Here's the pass . . . complete at the Grizzly 27, and Lardelle steps out of bounds!"

"Hey, the Grizzlies weren't expecting that, Don! Now the Wildcats have a first and 10 on the 27 with the clock stopped. I mean, giving up 5 or 10 yards is one thing, but the Grizzles gave the Kid enough room to take 15! Here comes kicker Ian Wallace to try for the winning field goal."

"Check out Brad Tacker, Don! And Rusty Kunkel and Olaf Hemingway! I've never seen those Grizzlies so mad! They were so sure of overtime that the 'Purple Wallop' got stung!"

"This will be a 44-yard kick, Al. Todd Schumacher snaps to the Kid, who is holding. Ian Wallace's kick is up! It's . . . good!"

"The Wildcats win it, 17–14! What a game!"

WILDCATS WIN!

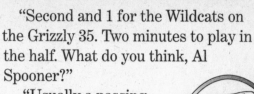

"Second and 1 for the Wildcats on the Grizzly 35. Two minutes to play in the half. What do you think, Al Spooner?"

"Usually a passing down, Don. And the Grizzlies see it that way too. The nickel defense is in."

"The Kid barks out the signals. Here's the snap. He hands off to Franco Turner. Turner takes it to the weak side, around left tackle. Safety Kevin Conn steps up to make the tackle . . . and *boom!* Turner runs right over him! He's finally dragged down at the 23 after a 12-yard gain and a first down!"

"That was a smart call, Don. You just don't want to go right at the strength of a defense. The Grizzlies are always tough to pass against, but in a nickel formation they are brutal."

The Wildcats drive for the touchdown, and the score is tied at halftime, 7–7. Now, with the third quarter drawing to a close, the Wildcat defense returns an interception for a touchdown.

"The Wildcats have taken their first lead of the game, 13–7. Here comes Ian Wallace into the game to try the extra point, Al Spooner."

"Sheepy Goodwin might have a trick up his sleeve here, Don. Let's watch."

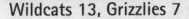

Quarter: 3	**Wildcats 13, Grizzlies 7**

Down: Conversion
To Go: 0
Ball on: Their 2
Time: 1:15
Defense: Stacked
Line

The kicking unit is in, but Ian Wallace has a message from your coach.

"Sheepy's wondering if we best be going for the two-point conversion, lad. I can kick for the one point, but he says it's your choice."

THE KID

Well, that's a thought. Sheepy probably thinks that if the game is going to be a defensive battle, you'd better try to get points when you can. Going for the two points would mean a pass to the tight end in the corner of the end zone, using the wide receivers as decoys. It's always a risk, especially against a defense as tough and smart as the Grizzlies'. And with Ian Wallace kicking, that one point is a pretty sure thing.

- To kick for one point, turn to page 38.
- To pass for two points, turn to page 26.

DON

"The Wildcat kicking unit is leaving the field, Al. It looks like the Kid will try for the two-point conversion."

"Brad Tacker sees something, Don. He's jamming Stubblefield and Jaeger right up to the line."

"Schumacher snaps the ball, and here come Stubblefield and Jaeger on the blitz! The Kid tries to throw quickly, but Jaeger tips it! Incomplete."

"Brad Tacker gambled that the Wildcats would pass, Don. With that kind of rush, there was no time for a pass play to develop."

AL

On the following kickoff, Ian Wallace reinjures his hamstring. The quarter ends with the Wildcats leading, 13–7. Early in the fourth quarter, the Grizzly offense drives for a touchdown and a 14–13 lead. Then, with less than two minutes to play, your offense starts to roll. You move to the Grizzly 49-yard line, where you face a third and 7.

"All right, Al Spooner. The Wildcat offense is finally moving again. They've crossed midfield, but they're down a point with only 1:05 to play and one timeout left."

"They may need that timeout now, Don. This is a passing down, and the Grizzlies are showing blitz!"

Quarter: 4   **Wildcats 13, Grizzlies 14**
Down: 3
To Go: 7
Ball on: Their 49
Time: 1:05
Defense: Blitz

THE KID

Check it out! Linebackers Andy Lee and Hank Stubblefield are lining up to blitz. You'll never get off a pass for 7 yards and the first down, so you'd better call an audible and change the play to a run.

A halfback *draw*, with you dropping back and handing off to Ray Rivera, might work. They won't be looking for a run, but a draw takes a little while to develop and it might get pretty crowded going through the line.

A *reverse* play, with you running right and handing off to Courtney Buckets heading left, could be the big play you need in this spot. It also takes a while for that kind of play to develop, but no linebacker or defensive end can catch Courtney once he gets going. Quick, decide!

- To run a halfback draw left, turn to page 37.
- To try a reverse left, turn to page 28.

"I'm telling you, Don, Brad Tacker doesn't mess around. He's going to blitz his boys and try to bury the Kid right here now!"

"Right you are, Al Spooner. The crowd is deafening! The Wildcats can barely hear the Kid's signals, but here's the snap."

"Here comes that 'Purple Wallop!'"

"The Kid fades right. Linebackers Hank Stubblefield and Andy Lee are closing in on him. But it's a reverse! The Kid hands the ball to Courtney Buckets, and now Buckets is running left! He eludes Andy Lee and defensive end Herb Grount and he's around the corner! Buckets is past the 40 . . . the 35 . . . the 25 . . . the 20 . . . and he's pushed out of bounds by safety Kevin Conn. First down, Wildcats, at the Grizzly 20. They're in easy field goal range with the clock stopped at 55 seconds and a timeout to spare!"

"Brad Tacker gambled on the rookie, but the Kid had him pegged, Don. Tacker and Grizzly coach Jack Rusk are talking on the sidelines. They look panicky. Rusk is putting in the *nickel* defense. Let's see what the Kid comes up with here."

Quarter: 4   **Wildcats 13, Grizzlies 14**

Down: 1
To Go: 10
Ball on: Their 20
Time: 0:55
Defense: Nickel

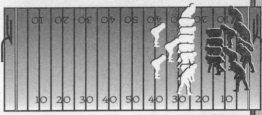

THE KID

That reverse shocked the Grizzlies. Now, call the right play and get it off quickly, because by the next down they'll be coming at you again.

You're within field goal range, but Ian Wallace is injured and can't kick. The Grizzlies don't know that, though. They're in a nickel formation to make sure they don't give up a touchdown, or let you get closer for an easier field goal. The secondary will keep the receivers in front of them. You could challenge them with Courtney Buckets on a long *hitch*, which would put you down near the goal line.

Or you could work on their linebackers (remember, in a nickel there are five defensive backs and just two linebackers) with a *draw* up the middle to Franco Turner.

- To pass to Buckets on a hitch, turn to page 30.
- To hand off to Turner on a draw, turn to page 34.

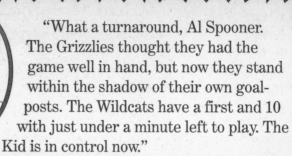

"What a turnaround, Al Spooner. The Grizzlies thought they had the game well in hand, but now they stand within the shadow of their own goalposts. The Wildcats have a first and 10 with just under a minute left to play. The Kid is in control now."

"I don't know how bad Ian Wallace hurt his leg, but the Wildcats are definitely in pretty easy field-goal range. The Grizzlies look like they're just playing it safe with their nickel defense in the game."

"The Kid fades back, and the Grizzly secondary drops back as well. Wide receivers Raj Sanders and Courtney Buckets are going deep, and the Kid throws . . . incomplete. The ball got batted down."

"Buckets was in front of double coverage."

"Long hitch pattern, Don, but it looked like the rookie, Emmitt Hood, got a hand on it. Now the clock is stopped, and the Kid has a second down and 10 to figure out."

"The Grizzlies have switched to a man-to-man defense, Don. Coach Jack Rusk seems to expect the Wildcats to run the ball up the middle two more times, and then bring in Ian Wallace for the winning field goal."

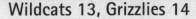
Quarter: 4   Wildcats 13, Grizzlies 14
Down: 2
To Go: 10
Ball on: Their 20
Time: 0:46
Defense: Man-to-Man
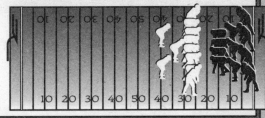

THE KID

Well, this is interesting. The Grizzlies are playing as if you're setting up for the field goal. They don't know that Ian is hurt! Maybe you can turn your disadvantage into an advantage and fool them. Give them something they'd never expect.

You could flood the secondary with receivers by sending halfback Ray Rivera and tight end Bobby Lardelle on pass routes. Maybe they'll bring up a safety to protect against the run and Courtney Buckets will be in single coverage.

Or you could send Courtney and Raj Sanders long to clear out the coverage and just hit Ray on a *fan* pattern to get you closer to the end zone. You've got 46 seconds, but don't *you* forget that Ian is hurt. It's going to take a touchdown to win.

- To pass deep to Buckets, turn to page 32.
- To pass to Rivera, turn to page 33.

"The Wildcats are probably going to run the clock down on the next two plays, then kick the field goal, Don. It looks like that's what Brad Tacker and the Grizzlies are thinking, anyway."

"Right you are, Al Spooner. And the Kid takes the snap from center. Halfback Ray Rivera drifts left out of the backfield, tight end Bobby Lardelle rolls off of Hank Stubblefield, wide receivers Raj Sanders and Courtney Buckets are breaking long! It's going to be a pass!"

"Linebacker Andy Lee is on Ray Rivera and middle linebacker Brad Tacker is covering Bobby Lardelle."

"The Kid puts it up for Buckets. Both he and Sanders are in double coverage. And it's . . . intercepted! O.B. Ballard picked it off! Buckets tackles Ballard on the spot."

"The Kid threw that one right into the coverage, Don. The Grizzlies have been double-teaming Buckets all day in their man-to-man defense."

"That's it, folks. The Grizzlies, with a 14–13 lead, will take over on offense and run out the clock."

GRIZZLIES WIN

"And now the Kid has two more tries before we see the field-goal unit."

"There's no way the Kid is going to take a chance on another pass like that, Don. This is easy field-goal distance, so the Kid is probably just going to hand off and work the clock down to skunk the Grizzly offense with no time after the kickoff. That's what Brad Tacker and the Grizzlies defense are getting ready for. "

"The Kid takes the snap, with Sanders and Buckets racing downfield. They're both taking defensive backs. But the Kid turns and throws to Ray Rivera. It's complete! And there's no one near him. Rivera turns for the end zone. It's going to be a foot race! Here comes Kevin Conn and Keith Jaeger! Rivera dives . . . touchdown!"

"Hey, Don, check this out: Clark Hashimoto is coming in to kick the extra point. Ian Wallace must be hurt worse than we thought. The kick is good, and the Wildcats take a 20–14 lead. And there's Grizzly coach Jack Rusk kicking the dirt over on the sideline. Sheepy and the Kid sure fooled him!"

WILDCATS WIN!

33

"The Grizzlies defense looks confused, Al Spooner, and the Kid isn't wasting any time taking advantage of it. How can anybody hear the signals in all this noise?"

"The Grizzlies put in a nickel formation, Don, and I think it's just to make sure they don't give up the quick touchdown pass. Man, they were all over this game, leading by one with the Wildcats iced at midfield! The Kid sure is something!"

"The Kid hands off to fullback Franco Turner up the middle. *Ouch!* What a block center Todd Schumacher put on Brad Tacker! Turner is loose in the defensive backfield. He picks up 11 yards, carrying safety Keith Jaeger on his back to the 9-yard line. First down and goal to go for the Wildcats!"

"Franco's looking strong, Don. He blew past both defensive tackle Olaf Hemingway and linebacker Hank Stubblefield. The Kid made a great call, but five yards of that was all Franco Turner!"

"The clock is ticking — 50 seconds, 49 .... The Wildcats call a timeout."

Down: 1
To Go: Goal
Ball on: Their 9
Time: 0:49
Defense: Man-
    to-Man

Timeout — your last one. You'd better go over and talk with Sheepy.

"You're doing great, Kid. The Grizzlies are going to stay in man-to-man and just keep reacting to whatever play you call. For just one play I'm going to send in Terry Warren for Courtney. If you see an opportunity, use him."

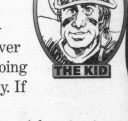

THE KID

You could send Terry Warren on a quick *out* pattern. He's great at shaking loose for the big catch, and the Grizzlies might try to cover him with just one man. It would stop the clock, and put you inside the 5.

Then again, they probably aren't looking for something like a power run down here. You could send Terry out on a decoy pattern, then send Franco Turner on a *sweep* right. You'd better call this one at the line, after you get a good look at the defense.

- To pass to Terry Warren, turn to page 36.
- To hand off to Franco Turner, turn to page 41.

"We have a substitution, Al Spooner. Veteran Terry Warren is in the game for Courtney Buckets. Does this signal a running play?"

"Could be, Don. But the Kid was jawing with Sheepy for a while. They might be up to something."

"Nine yards to glory for the Kid and the Wildcats. They step up to the line, with the Grizzlies in a man-to-man formation. The Kid bellows the signals over the din. Here's the snap."

"Raj Sanders is racing toward the end zone, with cornerback Ronnie Pepperidge on him. Linebackers Andy Lee and Hank Stubblefield are coming hard on a delayed blitz. The Kid throws to Terry Warren on a quick out inside the 5 . . . and it's *picked off!* Safety Keith Jaeger stepped in front of Warren for the interception. He falls with the ball, and Warren downs him there. What a terrible break for the Kid."

"That was a killer, man. But it was some great play by Keith Jaeger."

"And the Grizzlies take over, still leading 14–13. This game, folks, is history."

GRIZZLIES WIN

"We're down to the last minute of the game, Al Spooner, and the Grizzlies are looking to finish off the Wildcats here on third and 7 with a blitz."

"Last nail in the coffin, baby."

"The Kid steps up to center. Hike! It's a quick handoff to Ray Rivera on a draw play and . . . *splat!* Defensive tackle Rusty Kunkel stops Rivera at the line for no gain. The Wildcats use their last timeout to stop the clock."

"Another great play by the defense, Don. With all those linebackers blitzing, it was just too crowded in there for Rivera. And nobody blocked Rusty Kunkel. Look at him now! That old hog just found an acorn!"

"Now the Kid and the Wildcats face fourth and 7 at midfield with less than a minute to play."

Sorry, Kid. Fourth and seven is a passing down and the Grizzlies are in their nickel formation. You can't find an open receiver, so you dump a quick outlet pass to Ray Rivera, but it's good for only five yards. You lose the ball on downs. The Grizzlies, clinging to a 14–13 lead, run out the clock.

GRIZZLIES WIN

"After a moment's consideration, the Wildcats have decided to kick for the extra point, Al."

"They might as well take the sure thing."

"The Kid will hold for Ian Wallace, who hasn't missed on a conversion attempt all season. The kick is up . . . and it's good. The Wildcats take a seven-point lead."

"I think that was the smart choice, Don. Now, with the fourth quarter about to begin, the Grizzlies will have to put together two scoring drives to win, and they haven't been able to move the ball on the Wildcats since the first quarter."

The Grizzlies go nowhere on their next posses- sion and have to punt the ball back to the Wildcats.

"Okay, Al Spooner. The Wildcat offense is back on the field. They have excellent field position on the Grizzly 49-yard line."

"The Kid has a great chance to put this game away, Donald. There's still 13:25 to play, but the way the Wildcat defense has held the Grizzly offense, a two-touchdown lead would be a tough mountain to climb."

Down: 1
To Go: 10
Ball on: Their 49
Time: 13:25
Defense: Man-to-Man

THE KID

This is a pretty ordinary-looking down, Kid, but remember what your coach, Sheepy Goodwin, always says: "A football team doesn't win by looking for a handful of big plays, but by approaching every ordinary down as if it were a big play."

Maybe that means this would be a good time to go for it all. The Grizzlies are in a man-to-man defense; they aren't looking for the deep pass. Courtney Buckets could run a deep *fly* route. If he scores, you'd be up by two touchdowns.

But maybe it means that you should think of every down as part of the team's success. A one-play touchdown bomb and a five-play touchdown drive still both count for the same six points. And the drive would help use up the clock. What do you think?

- To pass deep to Buckets, turn to page 42.
- To pass short to the halfback, turn to page 40.

"On first and 10, just past midfield, these Wildcats are looking for a long drive to eat up as much of that clock as they can, Al Spooner."

"And the Grizzlies are looking to stop them, Don. It's still just a seven-point game. The Grizzlies are facing them in their straight up man-to-man formation. It's like they're saying 'Come on, baby, we're waiting! Take your best shot.'"

"Here we go! Todd Schumacher hikes to the Kid. Raj Sanders and Courtney Buckets are on medium crossing slant routes. Ray Rivera circles out of the backfield left. The Kid throws . . . and it's complete to Rivera! Tacker takes him down, but it's a big 15-yard gain! First and 10, Wildcats, at the Grizzly 34."

"That's what I call execution, Don. The Kid is in command."

The drive continues and the Wildcats score a touchdown on a run by Ray Rivera, to take a 21–7 lead. Scrambling to catch up, the Grizzly offense makes mistakes. The Wildcats won't score again, but a long drive will eat up the clock and end the game.

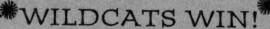

WILDCATS WIN!

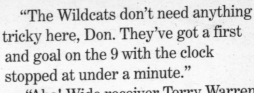

"The Wildcats don't need anything tricky here, Don. They've got a first and goal on the 9 with the clock stopped at under a minute."

"Aha! Wide receiver Terry Warren, the 13-year veteran, is in the game, Al. I wonder if the Grizzlies notice."

"They see him, Don. Keith Jaeger and O.B. Ballard are both lining up against him."

"The Kid takes the snap. Warren breaks right, but the Kid hands off to fullback Franco Turner. Left guard Larry Chapter pulls from the line and leads Turner on a sweep to the right! They turn the corner! Wilson Parker takes out Beardsley, Chapter blocks Stubblefield, Lardelle on Jaeger . . . touchdown! Franco Turner scores on a power sweep!"

"Great call! There was no way the Grizzlies were looking for a sweep! The fans are going crazy!"

Clark Hashimoto kicks the extra point for Ian Wallace, and then kicks off. The Wildcat defense holds the Grizzlies to protect the 20–14 lead, and time runs out.

WILDCATS WIN!

DON

"Here we go, Al Spooner. The Kid takes the snap. Courtney Buckets is on a deep fly route with O.B. Ballard step for step and Keith Jaeger a step behind! And here's the throw . . . incomplete!"

"That pass was just barely long, Don. But it was worth a try, I guess. A big play might have busted this game wide open. Instead, the Wildcats face a second and 10 from the Grizzly 49."

AL

The Wildcat drive stalls and Clark Hashimoto comes in to punt. Given a chance to get back into the game, the Grizzlies answer with a touchdown on the next drive to tie the score. Then, on the following drive, they kick a field goal to take a 17–14 lead. You get the ball back with just over four minutes left in the game. But you are sacked by Brad Tacker for a 4-yard loss and now you face a second down and 14 from your own 35-yard line.

"We're back live at the Metro Bowl, folks. And time is running out on the Wildcats."

"Hey, Don, don't forget that the Wildcats still have two timeouts. Now, it looks like the Grizzlies are putting in their *nickel* defense to guard against the long pass."

Down: 2
To Go: 14
Ball on: Your 35
Time: 3:40
Defense: Nickel

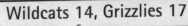

THE KID

This drive could be the game for you, Kid. The Grizzlies are pretty sure you're going to pass here, so they've brought in defensive back Emmitt Hood for linebacker Andy Lee in their nickel defense. Their secondary will be playing back, guarding against the first down pass. Both wide receivers will be double-covered, so this might be a good time to send tight end Bobby Lardelle over the middle on a medium *slant* pattern left.

But maybe a run would be safer. Right outside linebacker Hank Stubblefield is limping out there. Maybe a *trap* run by halfback Ray Rivera to the right side would work.

- To run Ray Rivera, turn to page 44.
- To pass to Bobby Lardelle, turn to page 50.

"The Grizzlies are looking to close the door on the Kid and the Wildcats here in the fourth quarter of Super Sunday, with under four minutes remaining to play. Don?"

"Schumacher hikes it, and the Kid hands off to halfback Ray Rivera. He breaks through the line . . . and linebacker Hank Stubblefield misses the tackle! Rivera is into the secondary! He's to the 40 . . . the 45 . . . the 50 . . . and he's finally brought down by safety Kevin Conn at the Grizzly 47! First down!"

"Great blocking by the Wildcat line, Don, and an outstanding run by Ray Rivera!"

The drive stalls at the Grizzly 20-yard line. The Wildcats have used up both of their timeouts and over two and a half minutes on the game clock on this drive.

"Do-or-die time for the Wildcats, Don. They have a fourth and 6 on the Grizzly 20 with just over a minute left to play. And they are not going to try for a field goal to tie. They are going in for the win. Either kicker Ian Wallace is hurt or this is one of the gutsiest calls I've ever seen. The clock is running and the Wildcats are going without a huddle."

44

Quarter: 4 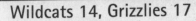 Wildcats 14, Grizzlies 17
Down: 4
To Go: 6
Ball on: Their 20
Time: 1:05
Defense: Nickel

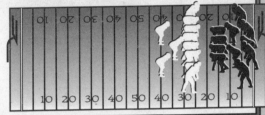

THE KID

No time to waste now, and no chance to go for the field goal with Ian hurt. You've got to get the first down and stop the clock.

An *out* pattern will probably work, but you've been going to Courtney Buckets all day. Maybe this time you should throw left to Raj Sanders.

Or since they're in a nickel, you could try a *sweep* right — left guard Larry Chapter pulling up from the line and running to the right, with Franco Turner, Wilson Parker, and Bobby Lardelle to lead the blocking for Ray Rivera — but that's a gamble on getting out of bounds, or even getting the first down. Make the call!

- To pass to Raj Sanders on an out, turn to page 49.
- To run Ray Rivera on a sweep, turn to page 46.

"The clock is running, with a minute left in this game, Al Spooner!"

"Fourth and 6 for the Wildcats at the Grizzly 20, the Grizzlies in a nickel, and the Wildcats can't stop the clock with a timeout!"

"The Kid takes the snap and hands off to Ray Rivera. Left guard Larry Chapter pulls to lead a sweep right! Wilson Parker, Bobby Lardelle, and Franco Turner out front. Rivera turns the corner! Wilson Parker just flattens Hank Stubblefield! Rivera is to the 15 ... the 10 ... and Brad Tacker knocks him out of bounds at the 4! First down and goal to go!"

"Whoa, baby, what a freight train!"

"The Metro Bowl is exploding with crazy Wildcat fans! That stops the clock at 55 seconds, and the Wildcats have new life!"

"You know, Don, the Wildcats have four downs to get these four yards, but this is no cinch deal. The Grizzlies are going to a *stacked line*, which is real tough to run against. And down here near the end zone, there isn't a lot of room for the Wildcat receivers to run pass patterns. Sheepy and the Kid are really going to have use their imaginations."

46

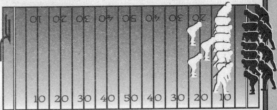

Quarter: 4   Wildcats 14, Grizzlies 17

Down: 1
To Go: Goal
Ball on: Their 4
Time: 0:55
Defense:
   Stacked Line

Okay, the Grizzlies are in a stacked line, so there's no way you'll be able to run on them for four yards. Besides, with no timeouts left, a run would use up too much time. Their pass coverage will be tight at this end of the field, but there are a couple things you could try.

THE KID

You could fake the handoff to Franco Turner, but send Ray Rivera on a *slip* left and pass to him in the end zone. Ray has to get open fast, though, because as soon as defensive backs Keith Jaeger and O.B. Ballard see what's happening, they're going to rush you.

Or you could send tight end Bobby Lardelle on a quick *hook* right. That would depend on Bobby getting away from linebacker Hank Stubblefield, and Courtney Buckets blocking O.B. Ballard out of the way. Okay, make the call.

- To pass to Ray on a slip left, turn to page 48.
- To pass to Bobby on a hook right, turn to page 53.

"It's pretty loud at that end of the Metro Bowl, Don, so it might be tough for the Kid to have those signals heard. I'm sure Sheepy Goodwin and the Kid already have a few plays called for this situation."

"The Kid takes the snap and hands off to Franco Turner . . . no! It's a fake! The Kid is looking left, where Ray Rivera is blocking Andy Lee, and here come O.B. Ballard and Keith Jaeger! *Ouch!* The Kid is sacked, and Jaeger knocks the ball loose. There's a scramble for the ball, Al Spooner, and a pileup. The refs are sorting it out. Both teams are signalling that they have possession, and the ball belongs to . . . the Grizzlies! The Grizzlies have escaped with a 17–14 victory."

"Tough break for the Wildcats, Don. It looked like the Kid was trying to toss it to Rivera after he crossed the line, but those linebackers had things too jammed up in there. Jack Rusk, Brad Tacker, and the rest of these Grizzlies are going to repeat as champions!"

GRIZZLIES WIN

"Here we go, Big Don. This is what championship football is all about!"

"Right you are, Al Spooner. Fourth and 6. There's 1:05 remaining, and the clock is running. Schumacher snaps the ball to the Kid. Courtney Buckets, double-teamed, is going long. Raj Sanders, also double-teamed, is running a short out, and the Kid throws to Sanders . . . but Emmitt Hood knocks it down. Incomplete!"

"That's the game, baby! The Kid was forcing it. He wanted the first down and to get Sanders out of bounds to stop the clock, but he threw right into nickel coverage. Maybe he forgot that in the nickel, the Grizzlies can put two defenders on Raj also.

"The Wildcats' title quest ends there, Al Spooner, as the Grizzly offense takes possession on downs. They'll run out the clock, with a 17–14 lead."

GRIZZLIES WIN

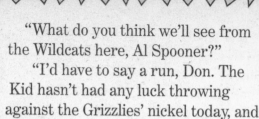

"What do you think we'll see from the Wildcats here, Al Spooner?"

"I'd have to say a run, Don. The Kid hasn't had any luck throwing against the Grizzlies' nickel today, and Terry Warren is in for Raj Sanders. That would say run to me."

"Okay, Al Spooner, except that the Kid is back to pass! Buckets and Warren are going long, taking four defenders with them. And Bobby Lardelle is cutting across the middle. The Kid hits Lardelle at the 50! First down, and Bobby is crossing the field and running down the left sideline. He's to the 40, and Kevin Conn pushes him out of bounds!"

"Whoa! How about that! Bobby Lardelle might not be fast, but he sure knew how to find the hole in that defense. Sheepy Goodwin and the Kid had everybody in this place fooled!"

The drive continues, working the clock down to near 2:00 and moving the ball inside the Grizzly 15.

"Time for one more play before the two-minute warning, Al Spooner."

"This is a great situation for the Wildcats, Don. They can get a first down without scoring, and they have two timeouts left plus the two-minute warning. The Grizzlies are in man-to-man."

Quarter: 4 **Wildcats 14, Grizzlies 17**

Down: 1
To Go: 10
Ball on: Their 12
Time: 2:10
Defense: Man-to-Man

You've got great field position, and the Grizzlies are ready for just about anything.

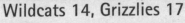

THE KID

You could hand off pretty safely here and give your receivers a short rest. Sending halfback Ray Rivera on a weakside run might catch the defense off balance.

Then again the Grizzlies are aware of your timeout situation and are probably looking for the run. Another pass might surprise them, especially if it's disguised as a run — maybe a pass to Franco Turner coming out of the backfield on a *checkthrough* right! Of course, in man-to-man it's the linebackers' job to stay with the running backs.

- To hand off to Ray Rivera, turn to page 61.
- To pass to Franco Turner, turn to page 52.

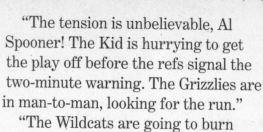

"The tension is unbelievable, Al Spooner! The Kid is hurrying to get the play off before the refs signal the two-minute warning. The Grizzlies are in man-to-man, looking for the run."

"The Wildcats are going to burn them with a pass, Don."

"There's the snap, and the Kid drops back. He fakes the handoff to Franco Turner. Turner has checked through the line on the right side! No one has picked him up. He's down to the five. The Kid passes . . . Turner's got it! He's over the goal line! Touchdown, Wildcats!"

"That was a brilliant pass play, disguised as a run! A perfect throw by the Kid and a great grab by Franco Turner! The Grizzlies looked like they were sure of the run, Don, or worse yet, like they thought the Wildcats were just waiting on the two-minute warning. Now the Wildcats take a 21–17 lead. It looks like heads-up, aggressive football by the Kid has just won a championship!"

WILDCATS WIN!

"Here we go, Don. It looks like Sheepy Goodwin is not even thinking about the field goal, the tie, and overtime. He just wants to win this thing and get out of here."

"We'll soon see, Al Spooner. The Kid takes the snap and fades back . . . it's going to be a pass! Tight end Bobby Lardelle rolls off of linebacker Hank Stubblefield, and wide receiver Courtney Buckets picks off O.B. Ballard. Lardelle is open at the goal line! The Kid throws . . . touchdown! The Wildcats go ahead with 50 seconds left in the game!"

"We didn't have to wait long, Al Spooner! Sheepy Goodwin and the Kid picked out just about the best play to run on this Grizzly goal-line defense! Lardelle got open at the goal line on a little quick hook set up by Courtney Buckets' block."

"The extra point is good! Now the pressure's back on the Grizzlies!"

The Wildcat defense holds on to clinch the 21–17 victory! Congratulations!

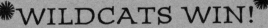

WILDCATS WIN!

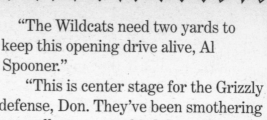

"The Wildcats need two yards to keep this opening drive alive, Al Spooner."

"This is center stage for the Grizzly defense, Don. They've been smothering teams all season on third down. They're so tough against the run."

"The Kid takes a short drop in the pocket. Ray Rivera and Franco Turner are blocking in the backfield. Now Turner rolls off linebacker Hank Stubblefield."

"It's a slip pattern!"

"The Kid passes . . . complete to Turner! Brad Tacker makes the tackle, but not before Turner picks up 10 yards and a first down at the Wildcat 38."

This drive leads to a touchdown, but the Grizzly defense shuts down the Wildcats for the rest of the first quarter. Fortunately, the Grizzly offense can't get anything going either. Late in the second quarter, a poor punt gives the ball to the Wildcats on your own 45-yard line. After three plays, you face a fourth down and inches to go for a first down.

"The clock is running, with 3:04 remaining in the half, Al Spooner. Let's see if the Wildcats are going to punt or go for it."

Down: 4
To Go: Inches
Ball on: Their 45
Time: 3:04
Defense: Stacked
   Line

You've got to choose carefully whether to punt or go for the first down.

The Grizzlies are just too tough up the middle to dive for the first down, so forget about that. You'll have to try something more clever. Maybe you can make it look like a *plunge*, then pass to fullback Franco Turner coming out of the backfield. If that fails, though, the Grizzlies will take over almost at midfield, with time to tie the score before the half.

THE KID

Maybe punting would be smarter. The Wildcat defense has done pretty well this half and you might get the ball back with enough time for a quick drive.

- To punt, turn to page 56.
- To pass to Franco Turner, turn to page 84.

"The Wildcats are going to play it safe on fourth down, Al Spooner. Here comes the punting unit."

"I have to question this call, Don. The Wildcats only need a couple of inches. If they don't get the first and turn the ball over here, so what? The Grizzly offense hasn't moved the ball all day!"

"Well, Al Spooner, I guess with a touchdown lead, the Wildcats would rather hand the ball over a little deeper in Grizzly territory."

"Clark Hashimoto booms a towering punt, driving Emmitt Hood back to the goal line. He crosses the 5 . . . the 10 . . . the 15 . . . . He breaks a tackle! He's at the 20 . . . and is finally brought down at the 25. And that's where the Grizzly offense will take over with 2:52 left in the first half."

The Grizzly offense drives 75 yards for a touchdown to tie the game, 7–7, at the half. The Wildcats kick off to the Grizzlies to start the second half, but the Grizzlies can't move the ball and punt it back to the Wildcats.

"Okay, Al Spooner, the Wildcats take over on offense on their own 30-yard line. The Grizzlies are in man-to-man. Let's see how the Kid decides to start out in the second half."

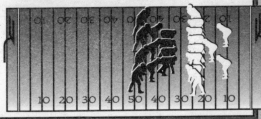

Down: 1
To Go: 10
Ball on: Your 30
Time: 12:50
Defense: Man-to-Man

THE KID

This is almost like starting a whole new game, isn't it? Except that you know a little bit about the Grizzlies now. What are they going to do on this play? They're in a man-to-man defense, which doesn't tell you much. Maybe they're waiting to see what you do.

If a smart and talented defense like the Grizzlies' is just going to react to your offense on a down, you need to take advantage of it. Man-to-man would put single coverage on Raj Sanders, and maybe he could beat his man deep. So how about a *post* pattern? It would sting them right off to start the half.

But then you never want to waste a play on a whim. Maybe it would be better to just go with a play that usually works — a short *hitch* pass to Bobby Lardelle, who will also be covered one-on-one.

- To pass short to Bobby Lardelle, turn to page 58.
- To pass deep to Raj Sanders, turn to page 74.

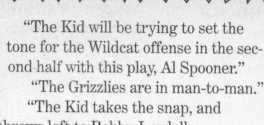

"The Kid will be trying to set the tone for the Wildcat offense in the second half with this play, Al Spooner."

"The Grizzlies are in man-to-man."

"The Kid takes the snap, and throws left to Bobby Lardelle, complete . . . and Kevin Conn hits him immediately!"

"*Boom!* I can't believe that Lardelle held on to the ball! That was some lick put on him by Conn."

"The pass was good for eight yards. Second and 2, Wildcats, at their own 38."

That little pass starts a long drive. Mixing up short and long passes and inside and outside runs, you drive to the Grizzly 15. Ian Wallace kicks a field goal to put you back ahead, 10–7. The two teams trade punts for the rest of the third quarter and into the fourth, when the Wildcats take over on their own 25-yard line.

"What a battle we have going on out here today, Al Spooner! We're still locked in a 10–7 thriller, with just a little over ten minutes to play."

"The Wildcats would love to start a drive here, Don. But the Grizzly defense also looks like they want to make something happen. The Kid steps up to the line, with first and 10."

Quarter: 4   Wildcats 10, Grizzlies 7

Down: 1
To Go: 10
Ball on: Your 25
Time: 10:10
Defense: Blitz

THE KID

    This is a dangerous situation, Kid. The Grizzlies believe that defense wins games, and they're going to try just that right here. Outside linebackers Andy Lee and Hank Stubblefield are up on the line — they're going to blitz.

    Do you remember how to beat a blitz? A reverse, a quick handoff inside, or a very quick pass. Forget about the reverse back here; a fumble would almost certainly lead to a Grizzly touchdown.

    A handoff, like a *trap* left, is always the safest option, but a quick pass could be interesting. You could send Ray Rivera on a *rim* route, but hit him with the ball just as he crosses the line of scrimmage. With Andy Lee blitzing, there would be no one to cover Ray. Okay, better call that audible.

- To pass to Ray Rivera, turn to page 60.
- To hand off to Ray Rivera, turn to page 62.

"The Grizzlies are showing blitz, Al Spooner."

"They're more like sharks than Grizzlies right now, Don. They're looking for blood!"

"The Kid comes up to the line. He looks around and barks out signals. It looks like he sees the blitz and is changing the play at the line. Todd Schumacher snaps the ball, and here come Andy Lee and Hank Stubblefield .... *Ouch!* The Kid is sacked and the ball is loose. Stubblefield falls on it, and Franco Turner downs him."

"Ray Rivera had trouble getting through the line. He was the intended receiver, but he just didn't get open fast enough."

"As it is, it's the Grizzlies' ball on the Wildcat 18, and it doesn't look good for the Kid, Al Spooner. He's not getting up. The Wildcat trainer is motioning for the stretcher."

Bad news, Kid. You've got a broken arm and you're out for the game. The Grizzly offense scores a touchdown off of the fumble, to lead 14–10, and without you the Wildcat offense cannot answer.

GRIZZLIES WIN

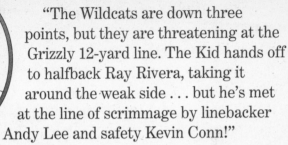

"The Wildcats are down three points, but they are threatening at the Grizzly 12-yard line. The Kid hands off to halfback Ray Rivera, taking it around the weak side . . . but he's met at the line of scrimmage by linebacker Andy Lee and safety Kevin Conn!"

"Fumble, baby!"

"The loose ball is scooped up by cornerback Ronnie Pepperidge and he's off to the races! He's to the 20 . . . the 25 . . . and brought down from behind by receiver Raj Sanders. Why were the Wildcats running the ball, Al Spooner?"

"I guess they thought they could change things up with a run, but it was such a no-doubt running play that the Grizzlies nailed it. No way was Brad Tacker going to mess up that call."

"And the Wildcat offense leaves the field. Trailing 17–14, their only hope is a miracle by the Wildcat defense."

Sorry, Kid. There are no miracles today.

GRIZZLIES WIN

"Don, would you look at Andy Lee and Hank Stubblefield! These Grizzlies are making no secret of the fact that they're planning to blitz. The Grizzly offense hasn't been getting it done, so it seems to be up to the defense to make the big play happen."

"Thanks, Al. There are just over 10 minutes to play in this championship contest, as the Wildcats step up to their own 25. The Kid barks out signals. Here's the snap . . . Lee and Stubblefield are coming . . . the Kid hands off to halfback Ray Rivera. Rivera slices past tackle Rusty Kunkel, tries to spin away from linebacker Brad Tacker . . . but Tacker hangs on and makes a shoestring tackle."

"That was a dandy 9-yard gain, Al Spooner. Nifty play-calling by the Kid to counter that dangerous Grizzly blitz."

You try to run against the Grizzly blitz again on second down, but this time Tacker stops Ray Rivera for no gain.

"Well, you can't go to the same well too often against this defense, Don. Now the Kid is facing a third and 1 from his own 34. The Grizzlies have a *stacked line* in the game. They expect another run."

Down: 3
To Go: 1
Ball on: Your 34
Time: 9:00
Defense: Stacked
    Line

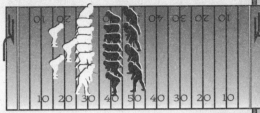

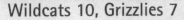

The Grizzlies are fighting you for every inch. If they hold you here they can get the ball back to give their offense another try.

They're in a stacked line formation, so it looks like they're expecting a *plunge.* You might make a plunge work by sending Raj Sanders and Courtney Buckets in motion as a distraction, and then having Larry Chapter and Todd Schumacher key on Rusty Kunkel, driving the line back to get Ray Rivera that yard.

You could also take a gamble on getting a receiver free of the cluster. Forget about Sanders and Buckets; the Grizzlies' secondary will be watching them too closely. Maybe tight end Bobby Lardelle can sneak open on a quick *out and fly.*

THE KID

- To run Ray Rivera on a plunge, turn to page 64.
- To pass to Bobby Lardelle, turn to page 68.

"The Wildcats line up in a tight formation. The Kid calls the sequence, Buckets and Sanders splitting wide. Here's the snap, and a handoff to Rivera. Rivera leaps . . . but he's met by linebacker Andy Lee in mid-air and pushed straight back!"

"I tell you, Don, you just can't try stuff like that against the Grizzly defense."

"The refs are marking it as a 2-yard loss, Al. And here comes Clark Hashimoto and the Wildcat punting unit."

Clark nails a nice punt, but Emmitt Hood takes it at the Grizzly 15-yard line and returns it 50 yards, to the Wildcat 35. The Grizzly offense scores a touchdown, and takes a 14–10 lead. Both teams are then unable to move the ball, but you get another chance in the final minutes of the game. You march the Wildcats downfield against the nickel defense with short passes. Now you have a first down on the Grizzy 25 with 1:15 to play and the clock running.

"The Grizzlies are still in the *nickel*, Don. Let's see what the Kid comes up with here. He'd better hurry."

Quarter: 4   Wildcats 10, Grizzlies 14

Down: 1
To Go: 10
Ball on: Their 25
Time: 1:15
Defense: Nickel

THE KID

You've got the Wildcats in great position, Kid. Now all you have to do is put the ball in the end zone.

If they're going to give you the short ones, you might as well take them. How about a medium *out and fly* to tight end Bobby Lardelle? Bobby can watch the coverage and either head out of bounds or, if there's room, take it downfield along the sidelines.

But maybe now is the time to change things up and really put it to them with a long pass to Courtney Buckets on a *post* pattern!

- To pass deep to Buckets, turn to page 66.
- To pass medium-range to Lardelle, turn to page 67.

"The Kid has been passing these Wildcats down the field, Don, and the Grizzlies are still sticking with that nickel formation. The Wildcats have a first down on the Grizzly 25 and they still have one time out."

"The clock is down to 1:05. Here's the snap, and the Kid drops back deep in the pocket! It's going to be a long pass! Courtney Buckets has double coverage on him and he's flying toward the goal line on a deep post. Here's the pass . . . Buckets and Ballard leap . . . and Ballard comes down with the interception! He's across the 10 . . . the 15 . . . the 20 . . . it looks like this is the game . . . and Eric Stern takes him down at the 35-yard line!"

"Well, Don, the Kid went to his go-to guy, Courtney Buckets. You can't fault that, but this Grizzly defense is just too talented."

"And it's official now, Al. These Grizzlies, with a 14–10 edge, will win back-to-back championships."

GRIZZLIES WIN

"We're almost to the one-minute mark in the game, Al Spooner, with the Wildcats threatening, first and 10, at the Grizzly 25. The Kid is not going to call for a timeout!"

"The Kid's in control, Don. No need to use that timeout until they really need it."

"The Grizzlies have remained in the nickel defense throughout this drive, Al Spooner. I can't understand why they haven't been blitzing."

"If the Grizzlies gamble and get burned, that's the game. They'll give the Kid short gains, but this way they don't figure to give up a touchdown."

"Here we go! The Kid takes the snap. Raj Sanders sprints down the left sideline. Courtney Buckets is on a medium slant, also heading for the left sideline . . . and Bobby Lardelle is running an out pattern at the 15! He's wide open! The Kid throws . . . and it's complete! Lardelle turns for the end zone! There's nobody near him! The coverage is all on the left sideline! Lardelle is at the 10 . . . the 5 . . . Lardelle scores! The Wildcats, now up 17–14, have unseated the defending champions!"

WILDCATS WIN!

"The Grizzlies are setting up with their stacked line for this Wildcat third and 1, Al Spooner."

"The 'Purple Wallop' defense doesn't want to give up some easy dive over the line, Don."

"Here's the snap . . . and the Kid's dropping back to pass! Bobby Lardelle is wide open . . . complete! He's to the 45 . . . the 50 . . . into Grizzly territory. Safety Keith Jaeger pushes him out of bounds at the 30 after a 36-yard gain!"

"Don, the Kid completely fooled the Grizzlies! What a play! The Grizzlies just couldn't adjust in time."

"First and 10, Wildcats, at the Grizzly 30."

The Wildcat drive stalls at the Grizzly 5. Ian Wallace kicks a field goal to increase your lead to 13–7. The Wildcat defense holds the Grizzlies on their next possession, and they must punt the ball back to you. You pick up nine yards on a pass to Raj Sanders on first down.

"Okay, Al Spooner, the Wildcats have a chance to put this game away. The Kid is looking at a second and 1 situation on his own 30-yard line, with just five minutes left to play."

Quarter: 4 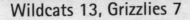 Wildcats 13, Grizzlies 7

Down: 2
To Go: 1
Ball on: Your 30
Time: 5:00
Defense: Nickel and Blitz

This is usually a good passing down, so the Grizzlies are in their *nickel* formation. But it looks a little different this time. Four of the defensive backs are positioned deep, guarding against the long gainer, but safety Keith Jaeger is much closer to the line. This looks like a *blitz* disguised as a nickel, and you can probably throw against it.

Time to call an audible. You could try Courtney Buckets on a *crossing* route in front of the coverage, or you could have Raj Sanders go long, then cut back on a *hitch* pattern.

- To pass short to Buckets, turn to page 73.
- To pass to Sanders, turn to page 70.

"Don, I see something tricky out there. The Grizzlies are in their nickel formation, but safety Keith Jaeger is right up on the line of scrimmage. It looks like he's going to blitz. Let's find out if the Kid sees what we see."

"The Kid takes the snap, drops back . . . and Jaeger *is* blitzing! Sanders starts going long, then stops and turns. The Kid tries to unload the ball and . . . *boom!* He released the ball just before Jaeger hit him, but the pass to Sanders was well short and incomplete."

The Wildcats fail to pick up the first down and must punt. The Grizzlies rally with a touch-down drive to take the lead, 14–13. You get the ball back and have one last chance to come up with some last minute heroics. You move the ball to your own 45-yard line. After a 1-yard run by Franco Turner that fooled no one, you now face a second and 9 with just 35 seconds to play.

"This game is not over yet, Al Spooner."

"That's true, Don. But the Kid and the Wildcats have a long way to go in a very short time."

Quarter: 4   Wildcats 13, Grizzlies 14
Down: 2
To Go: 9
Ball on: Your 45
Time: 0:35
Defense: Prevent

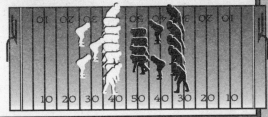

THE KID

This game is going to be decided by who's the smarter player, you or Brad Tacker. Now it's time for you to be very, very smart, so keep a cool head. The Grizzlies are in a prevent defense to guard against a touchdown. Okay, so you can't go long on them, but they'll give you the short stuff.

A run by halfback Ray Rivera would eat up time, not cover as many yards as a pass, and possibly cost you a timeout, but they aren't looking for the run.

A pass to Raj Sanders on a medium *hook* route would get more yards, and maybe stop the clock if he can get out of bounds. But the Grizzlies are really thinking pass right now. Remember: You don't need a touchdown to win.

- To run Ray Rivera on a trap left, turn to page 72.
- To pass to Raj Sanders, turn to page 77.

71

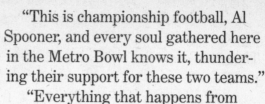

"This is championship football, Al Spooner, and every soul gathered here in the Metro Bowl knows it, thundering their support for these two teams."

"Everything that happens from here on out is crucial, Don. One missed assignment, one wasted play, will blow the game."

"The Kid and the Wildcats step up to their own 45 on second and one with just 35 seconds remaining in the game."

"Here's the snap, the Kid hands off to Ray Rivera, and he cuts through the line! He's over the 50 . . . the 45 . . . and linebacker Andy Lee takes him down at the Grizzly 41. First down."

"The Kid calls the Wildcats' last time out."

It was a great run, but you are now out of time outs and still about 15 yards beyond field goal range. You are able to move the ball another 9 yards, but with just 15 seconds left, and trailing 14–13, you must try for the field goal. Ian Wallace's 49-yard kick is wide to the left, no good.

GRIZZLIES WIN

"Second and 1 and the Kid's passing has been flawless all day, Don. These Grizzlies are looking for the pass here."

"There's the snap, and Keith Jaeger is blitzing! The Kid dumps it over the middle to Courtney Buckets! He's past linebacker Brad Tacker . . . Andy Lee misses him. Buckets is to the 35 . . . the 40 . . . and Kevin Conn snags him at the 45. A 15-yard gain!"

"Don, the Kid handled that like a 10-year veteran. The 'Purple Wallop' had disguised a safety blitz as just another ordinary nickel formation. It was a crafty call, but the Kid picked up on it."

"Now the Wildcats have a first and 10 almost at midfield and we're under five minutes in the game. It's looking pretty good for them."

The drive continues with short passes and clever handoffs. You score a touchdown on a quarterback sneak with just over two minutes left in the game to make the final score 20–7.

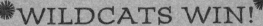

WILDCATS WIN!

73

"Here's the first snap of the second half for the Wildcat offense. The Kid drops back to pass. Raj Sanders is going deep! He's got Ronnie Pepperidge beat by a step! Here's the throw . . . incomplete!"

"But there are yellow flags all over the field, Don!"

"You're right, Al. Pepperidge had to grab Sanders just before that ball arrived or he would have scored a touchdown. That's pass interference. The Wildcats will get the ball on the Grizzly 30."

"Smart call by the Kid. He knew the Grizzlies expected Courtney Buckets to be the deep threat. So he went to Sanders, who was being guarded by only one defender.

That heads-up play leads to a Wildcat touchdown and a 14–7 lead! It will hold through the third quarter and into the fourth, when you get another scoring opportunity.

"The Wildcat offensive unit returns with great field position at the Grizzly 45. It looks like the Grizzlies are staying in man-to-man, trailing by a touchdown. What do you make of it, Al Spooner?"

"I'd say they're up to something, Don. Brad Tacker knows that the Kid can beat them deep."

Down: 1
To Go: 10
Ball on: Their 45
Time: 9:20
Defense: Man-to-Man

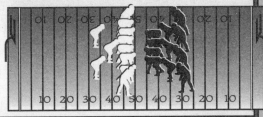

You were going to throw long against this man-to-man defense, but you'd better take a closer look at the line of scrimmage. Yes, you were right. The Grizzlies are going to shift from man-to-man to put double coverage on Buckets and Sanders. Safety Kevin Conn is going to help out Ronnie Pepperidge on Raj.

THE KID

This is a good running situation, maybe for handing off to fullback Franco Turner on a *draw* left. Or, if you feel like taking the gamble, you could try a pass to a receiver they aren't expecting you to throw to, like tight end Bobby Lardelle on a deep *post* pattern.

- To hand off to Franco Turner, turn page 78.
- To pass deep to Bobby Lardelle, turn to page 76.

DON

"Right you are, Al Spooner, the Grizzly secondary shifts, putting two backs on Buckets and two on Sanders. Todd Schumacher snaps the ball, and the Kid drops back into the pocket. Courtney Buckets is going deep . . . and Bobby Lardelle is wide open at the 25!"

"The Kid's gonna let it fly, Don! Here it comes!"

"Complete! Complete to Bobby Lardelle, over the 15 . . . the 10 . . . the 5 . . . touchdown, Wildcats!"

AL

"What a play, Don! Nobody was on Lardelle! The Kid beat their shift!"

"And the Wildcats take a commanding two-touchdown lead."

Trailing 21–7, the Grizzly defense will have to gamble on almost every down, trying to make something happen to force a turnover. You take advantage of that, passing to secondary receivers and to your backs on short patterns that turn into long gainers. The Grizzly offense narrows the margin to 24–14, but the . . .

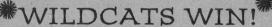

WILDCATS WIN!

"This is pressure football, Don. Trying to direct a game-winning drive in the thundering chaos of the Metro Bowl is enough to test the cool of a veteran quarterback, let alone a rookie."

"The Grizzlies are in their prevent defense with defensive backs Pepperidge, Conn, Hood, and Ballard standing back behind the 30, and Keith Jaeger all the way back behind the 10.

"Here's the snap. The Kid takes a short drop in the pocket, with no real pass rush. He throws . . . complete to Sanders at the 35, and Raj runs out of bounds to stop the clock. First and 10 for the Wildcats with just 29 seconds left."

"Smart call by the Kid. The Grizzly secondary was just keeping Buckets and Sanders in front of them, and he took what the defense gave him."

You continue to move the ball, on short plays, down to the Grizzly 26. With 14 seconds left in the game, the field-goal unit comes in. Ian Wallace's 43-yard kick puts you ahead to stay, 16–14!

WILDCATS WIN!

77

"The Wildcats come up to the line, Don, and the Grizzly secondary is shifting over. This is like a *nickel* now, two backs on Courtney Buckets, and two over on Raj Sanders."

"The Kid hands off to Franco Turner, a little draw play behind guard Larry Chapter. He's met by Brad Tacker and pulled down after just a 2-yard gain. Second down and 8."

"The Wildcats have got to do better than a draw play, even when the Grizzlies are in a nickel."

The Grizzly defense holds, and the Wildcats have to punt. Inspired, the Grizzly offense mounts a touchdown drive to tie the game at 14. Now, you're moving the ball late in the fourth quarter. After starting on your own 27, you beat the Grizzly blitz and nickel by throwing short passes. You're down to the Grizzly 30. The clock is stopped with just over four minutes to play.

"This is what championship football is all about, Al Spooner!"

"You got that right, Don! The Grizzlies aren't taking any chances now against the Kid; they're just staying in a man-to-man formation."

Down: 1
To Go: 10
Ball on: Their 30
Time: 4:05
Defense: Man-to-
     Man

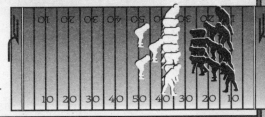

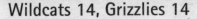

Now don't panic, Kid! There's lots of time on the clock. You just have to keep doing what you're doing, nothing fancy, just smart ball-control offense. Remember, a field goal will put you ahead.

THE KID

Maybe it's time to hit your go-to guy, Courtney Buckets. A high-percentage pass like a medium *out* might be good.

Then again, you've been passing a lot, so maybe a run would work. Better yet, maybe a concealed run, making it look like Franco up the middle, but you keep it instead and go around the *weak side* (the side the tight end is not lined up on).

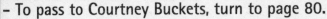

- To pass to Courtney Buckets, turn to page 80.
- To run a keeper yourself, turn to page 83.

"The Kid brings the Wildcats to the line, and Brad Tacker urges the Grizzly fans to make even more noise, Al Spooner."

"You know, Don, it seems to me that with a first down and this kind of field position, the Kid might want to eat up some of that clock. A field goal puts them up and they're already pretty much in Ian Wallace's range."

"The Kid takes a short drop, looks left to Raj Sanders, looks right to Courtney Buckets . . . and throws complete to the right sideline. Ballard gives Buckets a shot, pushing him out of bounds at the 15. Another Wildcat first down!"

The short passes keep working and in two plays you score a touchdown to take a 21–14 lead. But taking over the ball with plenty of time left and two timeouts, the Grizzlies answer with a touchdown of their own. What's worse, they score a two-point conversion! You take over again at your own 30, with only 55 seconds to play and move to the Grizzly 40. There you face a third down and 5.

"The Wildcats are battling back valiantly, Al Spooner. But the drive may be stalling here. This could be the game!"

Down: 3
To Go: 5
Ball on: Their 40
Time: 0:30
Defense: Man-to-
Man

Alright, the Grizzlies are in man-to-man. They aren't going to gamble with a blitz with the game on the line. They're going to play you for the pass or the run.

THE KID

You could surprise them with a pass to halfback Ray Rivera on a *rim* route for more than the first down. Ray might be able to break loose, but if he doesn't score or get out of bounds, you lose.

You could also go for a pass in front of their coverage, six yards and out of bounds. You could try Courtney Buckets on a short *hook* pattern.

- To pass short to Buckets, turn to page 82.
- To pass to Rivera for the score, turn to page 93.

DON

"The clock is running, with 30 seconds to play. The Grizzlies are in a man-to-man defense as the Wildcats come to the line, Al Spooner."

"Cornerback Ronnie Pepperidge is lining up tight on Raj Sanders. O.B. Ballard is showing Buckets a little more respect playing five yards back. Keith Jaeger and Kevin Conn are both playing pretty shallow."

"Here's the snap! The Kid takes a short drop. Buckets is double covered. The Kid throws anyway . . . and it is picked off by Keith Jaeger! Jaeger returns the ball to the 40 . . . the 45 . . . and Ray Rivera pushes him out of bounds at midfield."

"Keith Jaeger stepped in front of Courtney Bucket's hook route for the interception. I guess that's why he's all-pro, Al Spooner."

"The Kid was trying to force something, Don. The Grizzlies were looking for the pass on third and 5."

"Now, ahead 22–21, all that's left is for the Grizzly offense to run out the clock. Watch your tail, Grizzly coach Jack Rusk, you got a Gatorade shower coming!"

AL

GRIZZLIES WIN

"If I were Brad Tacker, I'd be looking for a run here, Don. The Wildcats will want to use up some clock before they score."

"Here's the snap, Al Spooner. The Kid hands off to Turner. He runs right into Grizzly linebackers Tacker and Lee . . . but wait, the Kid still has the ball. He's taking it around the left side! There's nobody near him! The Kid crosses the 20. Safety Kevin Conn is trying to catch him. This is going to be a foot race to the end zone. The Kid is to the 10 . . . the 5 . . . he dives forward . . . touchdown, Wildcats!"

"Wow! The Kid completely fooled the Grizzlies. The Kid is being mobbed in the end zone by his teammates. Todd Schumacher's squeezing him so hard, I'm afraid he's going to kill the poor guy."

"Todd had better be careful, Don. The Wildcats may still need the Kid. There's more than three minutes left to play."

No problem. On the next possession, the fired-up Wildcat defense stops the Grizzly offense on downs. You run out the clock for a 21–14 victory .

WILDCATS WIN!

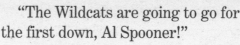

"The Wildcats are going to go for the first down, Al Spooner!"

"Well, the Grizzly defense led the league this year in allowing the fewest points scored, Don, so I don't blame the Wildcats. They've got to get the points where they can get 'em."

"The Kid steps up behind center Todd Schumacher. Here's the snap. The Kid's dropping back in the pocket! It's going to be a pass! The secondary splits to cover the receivers. Franco Turner is open coming out of the backfield! The Kid spots him at the 40 and throws . . . complete! Franco turns upfield, but Keith Jaeger takes him down at the Grizzly 35. First and 10, Wildcats!"

You finish out the first half by throwing a touchdown pass to backup wide receiver Terry Warren, to take a 14–0 lead. The Grizzly offense drives into Wildcat territory to start the third quarter, but fumbles at the 31. You take over there. But an incomplete pass on first down and a 4-yard run on second leaves you in a hole.

"That Grizzly turnover still may be costly, Don, but now the Wildcats seem to be stuck on their own 35, with a third and 6. That can be a lot of turf to cover against the Grizzlies."

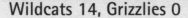

Quarter: 3   Wildcats 14, Grizzlies 0

Down: 3
To Go: 6
Ball on: Your 35
Time: 13:25
Defense: Man-to-Man

The Grizzlies are in man-to-man. They aren't risking a big gain on a pass with a blitz and they aren't risking the first down on a run with a nickel. But by playing it safe, they can be beat anyway, if you call the right play.

THE KID

You could go with thunder, handing off to fullback Franco Turner on a *trap* right. Or you could go with lightning, and send Courtney Buckets on a long *fly* against double coverage. You need to get something started and Courtney is your best receiver. Just be sure to throw a lead pass, and give Courtney time to run under it.

- To hand off to Franco Turner, turn to page 86.
- To pass deep to Courtney Buckets, turn to page 89.

"The Kid sets up under center. Here's the snap . . . and it's a handoff to Franco Turner on a trap right. Turner is brought down by Brad Tacker after a 4-yard gain."

"That's not enough for the first down, Don, and here comes the Wildcat punting unit."

The Grizzly offense puts together a long touchdown drive on their next possession, and then scores a field goal on the following possession to narrow the Wildcat lead to 14–10. Meanwhile, the Grizzly defense continues to shut down the Wildcat offense. On a Wildcat possession midway through the fourth quarter, the Grizzly "D" tries to turn the game around completely. You try a handoff for no gain on first down, and then you're sacked by Brad Tacker for a 5-yard loss on second down.

"The Kid will have to get something going here if he hopes to win this game, Al Spooner."

"The Wildcats are on their own 25, facing third and 15. The Grizzlies are in their *nickel* defense, looking to stop the pass."

Down: 3
To Go: 15
Ball on: Your 25
Time: 8:40
Defense: Nickel

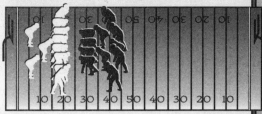

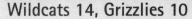

THE KID

Everybody is expecting a pass here. That means you should do the unexpected. Raj Sanders will be in double coverage and Courtney Buckets will also have two defenders on him.

A pass can work if it's to a running back. If you send Courtney long, it will clear the defenders out on the right side. Since a pass to the halfback is the most typical here (the halfback is usually faster), you could surprise them with a toss to fullback Franco Turner in the flat and let him try for the first down.

Or you could really surprise them by keeping the ball yourself and running a *draw*. They wouldn't be expecting that, and you might get past them so quickly that you could pick up the first down.

- To pass to fullback Franco Turner, turn to page 90.
- To run the ball yourself, turn to page 88.

"The pressure is on the Kid now, Donald. It will be tough to get the first down against the Grizzlies' nickel defense. We've seen that all day."

"The Kid steps up behind center Todd Schumacher, with Sanders and Buckets both split wide. Schumacher hikes it. Both wide receivers are breaking long . . . but the Kid is keeping it! He's through the line. He's to the 35 for the first down! The Kid picks up a block and crosses midfield. Emmitt Hood makes a grab at him . . . but the Kid laterals to Ray Rivera! Rivera is to the 40 . . . the 30 . . . the 20 . . . he's gone! Touchdown, Wildcats!"

"A great play! The Grizzlies weren't expecting a quarterback keeper, and they certainly weren't looking for Rivera trailing for the lateral!"

"Most of the fans here are stunned. The Kid has put the Wildcats back in control, 21–10!"

Great play, Kid! The Grizzly defense will hold you scoreless for the rest of the game, but the Grizzly offense is so shocked that they can't move the ball. Your 11-point margin will stand.

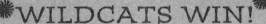

WILDCATS WIN!

"The Grizzlies are in man-to-man coverage. The Wildcats step up to the line. The Kid takes the snap and steps back into the pocket. There's a lot of pressure from the Grizzly pass rush. The Kid winds up to throw! Buckets has his men beat at the Grizzly 45! The Kid throws . . . complete! Buckets has a step on both Ballard and Jaeger at the 35. He's to the 30 . . . the 25 . . . he's going to score . . . the 15 . . . 10 . . . 5 . . . touchdown!"

"The Kid threw a perfect pass, Don, and we just saw how dangerous Courtney Buckets is. On a good lead pass, double coverage isn't going to stop him."

The Grizzlies put triple coverage on Courtney Buckets, and you are able to pass to Raj Sanders and Bobby Lardelle the rest of the way. Things also open up for the Wildcat running game. You score another touchdown in the third quarter, and a field goal in the fourth to blow out the Grizzlies and win the championship, 31–7!

WILDCATS WIN!

"The Kid calls the signals and Schumacher snaps the ball. The wide receivers are going deep. The Kid drops back . . . and lobs a pass to Franco Turner in the right flat. Turner crosses the line of scrimmage . . . and *crunch!* Hank Stubblefield nails him at the 27. Two-yard gain, and it's fourth and 13. Clark Hashimoto will have to punt it away."

Clark nails a great punt, but it won't matter. The Grizzly offense marches 85 yards and scores a touchdown to take a 17–14 lead. You and the Grizzlies exchange punts, and you get the ball back at your 40 with a minute left. Four quick passes take you all the way to the Grizzly 30.

"The clock is stopped at four seconds, Al Spooner! This is what championship football is all about!"

"The Metro Bowl is rocking, Don. The Kid is screaming to be heard in the huddle. The Wildcats are on the edge of Ian Wallace's range, so they're going to have but one last play to win or lose this game. Here we go, baby!"

Quarter: 4   Wildcats 14, Grizzlies 17

Down: 1
To Go: 10
Ball on: Their 30
Time: 0:04
Defense: Prevent

THE KID

It comes down to this one play, Kid. They know you're going to pass, but you've got no choice.

Courtney Buckets is the best you've got. You could send him deep into the coverage, then have him *hitch* back and hope he comes down with the ball in the end zone.

Or you could bring in Terry Warren and throw to him on a deep *fly* left. Maybe the Grizzlies would be worrying so much about Buckets that they wouldn't notice him coming into the game. He isn't as fast as he was, but he runs good routes. Make the call. Make it happen.

- To pass to Courtney Buckets, turn to page 92.
- To pass to Terry Warren, turn to page 94.

91

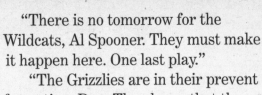

"There is no tomorrow for the Wildcats, Al Spooner. They must make it happen here. One last play."

"The Grizzlies are in their prevent formation, Don. They know that the Kid has to pass. This isn't going to be easy for the Wildcats."

"And the Wildcats come to the line amid the deafening roar of the crowd. The Kid steps up behind center Todd Schumacher. Schumacher snaps the ball. The Kid drops back, the wide receivers are going deep! The Kid is watching Courtney Buckets. The Kid pumps once, then throws deep! The pass is in the air for Buckets! This is going to be a jump ball in the end zone, and the pass is . . . batted away! All-pro Keith Jaeger knocked the pass down!

"The game is over! The Grizzlies win, 17–14!"

"Man, what a game! It's a tough way for the Kid's great season to end, Don. But nobody has to hang their heads, especially the Kid. These Wildcats put up a valiant fight, but the defending champion Grizzlies were just too tough today."

GRIZZLIES WIN

"The Grizzlies are in man-to-man, with the secondary playing fairly close to the line, Don. They don't want to give up a first-down pass here."

"Here's the snap, and the Kid drops back. Sanders and Buckets are both covered tight. But there goes Ray Rivera out of the backfield! He's breaking long! The Kid throws, and the pass is complete at the 30-yard line. Rivera is to the 25 . . . the 10 . . . the 5 . . . touchdown, Wildcats!"

"Wowee, baby! The Wildcats have taken the lead with just 22 seconds remaining! Sheepy Goodwin is on the field hugging the Kid! This crowd is going nuts! Don, this has been the best championship game I've ever seen!"

The extra point makes the score 28–22. Time runs out on the Grizzly offense.

WILDCATS WIN!

"The noise of this crowd is deafening, Don. The Kid is screaming out the call. This is it! One last play!"

"Schumacher hikes it. The Kid drops back, the wide receivers are going deep! Courtney Buckets is running into triple coverage: Hank Stubblefield is back waiting with Jaeger and Ballard. And, wait a minute, that's Terry Warren on the other side!"

"I didn't see Warren come into the game, Don!"

"The secondary on the left side is drifting over toward Buckets . . . and the Kid throws to Terry Warren! It's complete at the 5. Touchdown!"

"I don't believe it! Just like that, the Wildcats win, 20–17, on a last second bomb to Terry Warren. The Kid has turned that old warhorse into a hero!"

"The fans are rushing onto the field! Time has expired. The refs and the state patrol are trying to contain this pandemonium!"

"Don, I'm heading down to the Wildcats locker room for the trophy presentation, and I've got to talk to the Kid! He's the MVP in my book."

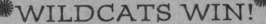

WILDCATS WIN!